Silent Frights

Silent Frights

Matthew Petchinsky

Silent Frights: A Collection of Christmas Creepypastas to Chill Your Bones

By: Matthew Petchinsky

1.The Red Stocking Ritual

It started as a whispered dare passed around middle school halls: a game no one truly believed, until someone tried it. They said if you followed the instructions exactly, something *otherworldly* would answer your call on Christmas Eve. They called it the "Red Stocking Ritual."

I never believed in that sort of thing. Ghosts? Demons? Urban legends? Just fuel for creepy YouTube videos. But this year, something about the holidays felt... hollow. My parents were working late shifts, and it was my first Christmas Eve alone in our big, drafty house. So, out of boredom—or maybe desperation for some excitement—I decided to give it a shot.

The rules were simple but specific:

1. Hang a red stocking (it must be red) above a fireplace or on your door handle if you don't have a chimney.
2. At exactly 11:11 PM, write down your deepest Christmas wish on a piece of paper. It must be a wish for someone else, not yourself.
3. Fold the paper three times, place it in the stocking, and whisper, "Saint Nicholas, hear my plea. Deliver this wish, I beg of thee."
4. Turn off all the lights and sit in silence for 11 minutes. Do not move, no matter what you hear.

I hung the stocking on my bedroom door. I didn't have a fireplace, so this would have to do. At 11:11 PM, I scribbled my wish—something dumb like wishing my parents could have the holiday off next year—and slipped it into the stocking. My voice wavered as I whispered the words, suddenly feeling childish.

Then, I turned off the lights.

The first few minutes were uneventful, just the hum of my space heater and the faint tick of my wall clock. But as the seconds dragged on, the air in the room grew colder—unnaturally cold. The heater clicked off without warning, leaving an eerie silence.

I told myself it was just my imagination.

Then came the sound.

It started as a faint scratching, like fingernails against wood. I froze, heart hammering, but reminded myself of the rule: **Do not move, no matter what you hear.**

The scratching grew louder, more insistent, like something—or someone—was clawing at the other side of my bedroom door. My breath caught in my throat as I saw the red stocking sway back and forth, though there was no draft.

And then the whispering began.

It was soft at first, indistinct murmurs that I couldn't understand. But as the whispers grew louder, they became clearer—voices, many voices, speaking in unison. They repeated my wish back to me, over and over, in a mocking sing-song tone.

"Saint Nicholas, hear my plea. Deliver this wish, I beg of thee."

I clenched my fists, fighting the urge to scream. The voices stopped, replaced by a low, guttural chuckle that came from the other side of the door. My eyes darted to the clock—11:22 PM. The ritual was over. I should've been safe.

Then why wasn't it stopping?

The door handle rattled violently. The scratching turned to pounding, as if something massive was trying to break in. The red stocking tore loose and fell to the floor.

And then everything stopped.

Silence.

I didn't dare move. I didn't breathe. But curiosity got the better of me, and I reached for my flashlight. When I clicked it on, the room looked normal—too normal. The stocking was back on the door handle, as if it had never fallen.

I crept toward it, trembling. Inside was the folded piece of paper I had written my wish on. Only now, there was something else.

I pulled it out—a small, shiny object. A candy cane, its stripes glistening unnaturally red. I stared at it, confused, until I noticed the paper. My handwriting had changed. My innocent wish was gone, replaced by a single sentence written in a spidery scrawl:

"One wish granted, one price paid. Enjoy your *gift*."

The candy cane broke apart in my hand, crumbling into a fine, sticky dust that smelled like copper.

The next morning, I found out my parents' car had slid off an icy road on their way home. They survived, but barely. The doctors said it was a miracle.

But I know better.

I tried to destroy the stocking, but no matter what I do, it always reappears—on my door, above the fireplace, even in my closet. And every Christmas Eve, the scratching begins again.

This year, I'm begging you: **don't try the Red Stocking Ritual.** It doesn't grant wishes. It only takes.

2.The Christmas Caller

Every Christmas Eve, my family had a tradition: we'd turn off all the lights except for the glow of the Christmas tree, sit by the fireplace, and tell holiday stories. But one year, everything changed.

It was the year we lost Grandma. She'd always been the heart of Christmas, baking cookies, singing carols, and wrapping presents in her perfectly neat, signature red bows. After she passed, my parents tried to keep the tradition alive, but it felt hollow. Still, we went through the motions.

That Christmas Eve, it was just me, my younger brother Jake, and my parents. The air felt heavy, the silence too loud even with the faint crackle of the fire. At exactly 11 PM, the phone rang.

We all froze. Who would call so late on Christmas Eve?

Dad answered, his voice cautious. "Hello?"

For a moment, there was no response. Then his expression changed—his face went pale. "Mom?" he whispered.

I stared at him. Grandma had been gone for six months.

Dad's voice quivered. "Mom, is that you?"

The rest of us huddled around him, straining to hear the other end of the line. There was a faint sound, like static or wind, and then a soft, familiar hum.

It was Grandma's voice, clear as day, humming her favorite carol: *Silent Night*.

Dad dropped the phone, and Jake scrambled to pick it up. "Grandma?" he asked, his voice trembling with both fear and hope.

"Jake," the voice said, low and warm, but slightly distorted. "You've been such a good boy this year. I've missed you."

Jake's eyes filled with tears. "We miss you too, Grandma. Are you... are you in heaven?"

There was a pause, followed by a chilling response: "Not quite."

The line went dead.

We stared at each other, unsure what to do. Mom, trying to calm us, said it must've been a prank or our imaginations. But deep down, we all knew what we'd heard.

That night, none of us slept well. I kept hearing faint whispers in the house, though I convinced myself it was the wind. Around 3 AM, I woke up to Jake shaking me.

"She's here," he whispered, his face pale.

"What are you talking about?" I hissed.

He pointed to the hallway. The faint glow of the Christmas tree reflected off the floorboards, and I could hear something—soft footsteps, slow and deliberate.

"Mom? Dad?" I called out.

No answer.

I got out of bed and crept toward the hallway, Jake clutching my arm. As we peeked around the corner, we saw her.

Grandma.

Or at least, it *looked* like her. She was standing by the Christmas tree, her back to us. She wore her favorite red sweater, the one she was buried in. Her hair was the same silver curls we remembered, but something was off. Her movements were jerky, almost mechanical, as she reached for an ornament on the tree.

"Grandma?" Jake whispered.

She turned her head slowly, too slowly, until we could see her face. Her eyes were hollow, dark pits, and her mouth stretched into a smile that was too wide, too sharp.

"You didn't finish your wish list," she said, her voice echoing unnaturally.

I grabbed Jake and bolted for my parents' room, slamming the door behind us. Dad woke up instantly, demanding to know what was wrong. When we told him, he grabbed the baseball bat from under his bed and went to check the house.

The living room was empty. No sign of Grandma—or whatever that thing was. But the phone was off the hook, and on the floor next to it was an ornament we'd never seen before: a tiny glass figurine of Grandma, smiling serenely.

We didn't finish Christmas that year. The tree came down the next morning, and we haven't put one up since. But every Christmas Eve, at exactly 11 PM, the phone rings.

We never answer.

And every year, we find another ornament in the house—another member of the family, perfectly preserved in glass, smiling that same unnatural smile.

We're running out of places to hide them.

3.The Gingerbread Golem

Every Christmas, our little town of Hearth Hollow held a gingerbread contest. Bakers from all over would compete to create the most elaborate gingerbread houses, men, and sculptures. The air smelled of cinnamon and sugar for days, and the winning creation was displayed in the town square until New Year's Day.

But last Christmas, everything changed when Old Man Griggs entered the competition.

Griggs wasn't a baker. He wasn't even the festive type. A recluse who lived in the woods on the edge of town, he rarely came to town meetings or spoke to anyone. No one expected him to show up at the contest. But when he did, dragging a tarp-covered cart behind him, everyone fell silent.

With a flourish, he yanked the tarp off to reveal his entry: a towering, seven-foot gingerbread man.

The thing was terrifying. Its body was jagged and uneven, like it had been hacked out of dough rather than carefully shaped. Its icing wasn't the cheerful white piped into snowflakes and swirls like the other entries—it looked more like veins running across the dark, molasses-colored body. Its eyes were sunken raisins, and its jagged, toothy grin was made from broken candy canes.

"I call it the Gingerbread Golem," Griggs said, his voice gravelly and dry.

No one clapped. No one moved. Even the mayor, who always gave warm words to every contestant, seemed lost for what to say.

Griggs didn't wait for applause. He left the golem there and walked out without a word.

That night, it started snowing heavily, blanketing the town in silence. I was walking home from a late shift at the diner when I passed the square. The contest entries were still on display, their sugar facades glowing faintly under the streetlights.

Except the Gingerbread Golem.

It was gone.

At first, I thought maybe Griggs had come back to take it, but then I noticed something. Deep footprints in the snow led away from where it had been standing—massive footprints, larger than any human could make.

I followed them.

They led down Main Street, past the bakery and the post office, and stopped in front of the mayor's house. The door was ajar, and the footprints continued inside.

I hesitated, my breath fogging in the freezing air. The house was dark except for the soft glow of Christmas lights in the window. I stepped closer, peering inside.

The living room was a mess. Furniture was overturned, the Christmas tree was on its side, and ornaments were shattered across the floor. In the center of the chaos was a trail of something thick and dark.

Molasses.

My stomach turned as I followed the trail upstairs, my heartbeat loud in my ears. At the top of the stairs, the mayor's bedroom door was open.

I didn't go in. I didn't need to.

The mayor was there—or what was left of him. His body was crushed, his limbs bent at impossible angles. His face was frozen in a scream, and his chest was caved in, as if something massive had stomped on him.

And in the corner of the room, written on the wall in thick, sticky molasses, was a single word:

"BAKE."

I ran out of the house and didn't stop until I was home. I locked every door and window and sat by the fire with a knife in my hand, waiting for morning.

By the time the sun rose, news of the mayor's death had spread through the town. No one talked about the footprints or the molasses. The official story was a break-in gone wrong, but I knew better.

That night, as the snow fell again, I heard something outside. A heavy, deliberate crunching of footsteps in the snow.

I peeked out the window and saw it.

The Gingerbread Golem, standing in my yard, its candy-cane grin gleaming in the moonlight.

In its hand was a note, scrawled in shaky, icing-like letters.

"Your turn."

Now, every Christmas Eve, I bake something. A gingerbread man, a house, anything to appease it. But each year, it gets closer.

And one day, I know it won't be satisfied with just a cookie.

4. The Night of Three Shadows

Our town, Winter Hollow, had always prided itself on being the most festive place in the country. Christmas lights adorned every building, carolers filled the streets, and the annual Christmas Eve parade was legendary. But last year, Christmas wasn't merry. Last year, it became a nightmare.

It started with a strange visitor—a drifter who called himself Klaus. He arrived weeks before the holiday, selling peculiar trinkets from a sleigh-like cart pulled by a single black goat. Klaus was pale, his eyes sharp as broken glass, and he spoke in a voice that sent chills down your spine, even when he smiled.

One day, Klaus stopped at the town square and began handing out free "gifts" to the children. Small carved figurines, each one uniquely grotesque—a horned devil, a monstrous gingerbread man, a twisted Santa with a skeletal grin. Parents protested, but Klaus laughed, saying, "Oh, don't worry. They'll all come to life on Christmas Eve."

Everyone thought it was a sick joke.

Until Christmas Eve.

The parade had just ended, the streets filled with laughter and music, when the first scream cut through the air.

I was with my younger sister, Lily, watching the fireworks, when the ground beneath us trembled. A thunderous roar echoed from the square, followed by the sound of splintering wood. We turned to see the massive Christmas tree collapsing, its lights flickering and dying.

And standing where the tree had been was the **Gingerbread Golem**.

It was twice the size of the one Old Man Griggs had made years ago, its jagged body covered in dark, dripping frosting. Its candy-cane teeth glistened red as it opened its maw and let out a guttural roar. People scattered as it began smashing everything in sight, its massive, cookie-frosted fists turning carts and lampposts into splinters.

As if that wasn't terrifying enough, a second figure emerged from the shadows. This one was tall and hulking, with fur-covered legs, curling black horns, and claws like daggers. **Krampus.** His chains rattled as he stalked through the panicked crowd, his long, forked tongue flicking out as he snatched children off the ground, stuffing them into a burlap sack slung over his shoulder.

Lily screamed and clung to me, but I couldn't move. My legs felt like jelly as a third figure stepped into view.

Santa Claus.

But this wasn't the jolly old man from storybooks. This Santa was a skeletal figure draped in tattered red robes, his beard matted and streaked with soot. His eyes burned like embers, and when he grinned, his teeth were yellowed fangs.

"Ho ho ho," he boomed, his voice hollow and echoing. "Have you all been good this year?"

No one answered. No one dared.

Santa's grin widened. "No? Well then, let's make this Christmas one to remember." He raised a gloved hand, and a fiery red light shot into the sky, exploding like a blood-stained star. The Gingerbread Golem and Krampus let out deafening howls, and chaos erupted.

I grabbed Lily's hand and ran, weaving through the screaming crowd. The Gingerbread Golem smashed through a row of shops like they were made of paper, and Krampus's sack squirmed with the cries of terrified children. Santa floated above the carnage, his skeletal sleigh pulled by eight black, decaying reindeer, their glowing eyes scanning for stragglers.

We made it to the church, one of the few stone buildings in town, and barricaded ourselves inside with a handful of others. For hours, we listened to the sounds of destruction outside—roars, screams, and Santa's hollow laughter echoing through the night.

By dawn, the town was unrecognizable. The square was a wasteland of broken decorations and ash. The Gingerbread Golem was gone, leaving only massive, crumbling footprints behind. Krampus's sack lay discarded, empty and stained with something dark. And Santa? He had vanished, leaving a single, charred sleigh bell in the center of the square.

We thought it was over.

Until we saw the gifts.

Every doorstep in Winter Hollow had a single present waiting for the family inside. Inside each box was one of Klaus's grotesque figurines, identical to the ones he had handed out weeks before. But now, they looked... alive. Their tiny eyes moved, their limbs twitched, and their mouths curled into sinister smiles.

No one dared touch them. No one dared throw them away.

This year, Klaus hasn't returned. But the figurines? They're still here, sitting on shelves, staring at us with their beady eyes. And as Christmas approaches, their grins seem to grow wider.

We know they're waiting.

For him.

5.The Grinning Gifter

It started as a rumor, a whispered urban legend among kids in my neighborhood. They called him **The Grinning Gifter**, a shadowy figure who appeared only during the twelve nights leading up to Christmas. If you found a gift on your doorstep with no tag and no explanation, you were supposed to open it immediately. If you didn't? Well, no one seemed to know what happened—only that no one who ignored the gift was ever seen again.

Of course, it was just a creepy story to scare kids into checking for packages. At least, that's what I told myself. But last year, on December 13th, I found the box.

It was sitting on my front porch, wrapped in bright red paper with a shimmering silver bow. There was no name, no card—just a simple tag that read: **"For You."** The paper was pristine, untouched by the frost-covered steps, and the bow seemed to glow faintly in the moonlight.

I hesitated, the legend suddenly coming to mind. It was stupid, I told myself. Just a prank from a neighbor. But as I picked up the box, I felt an odd warmth emanating from it, almost like it was alive.

I brought it inside and sat it on the kitchen table. My curiosity warred with my skepticism. After a few moments, I tore the paper off.

Inside was a small, hand-carved wooden figure of a man. His face was grotesquely exaggerated—a wide, toothy grin stretching from ear to ear, his hollow eyes staring straight through me. He wore a long red coat and a crooked hat, and his tiny, jointed hands held a perfectly wrapped gift. Something about him made my skin crawl.

Underneath the figure was a note, written in looping, ornate hand-writing:

"He gives, and he grins. Ignore him, and he wins."

I shoved the figure and the note back into the box, heart pounding. It had to be a prank—someone trying to scare me. I decided to throw it away, but when I opened the front door to toss it in the garbage, I froze.

The figure was standing on the porch.

Not in the box. Not in my hands. Standing upright on the porch, its carved grin wider, its hollow eyes fixed on me.

I slammed the door and locked it. My pulse raced as I backed away. When I turned around, the figure was on the kitchen table. Its tiny, wooden hands were now empty—the wrapped gift it had been holding was gone.

A knock at the door made me jump. Three slow, deliberate knocks. I didn't answer. I couldn't.

But then, I heard it.

The faint sound of wrapping paper tearing. It was coming from the living room.

I crept forward, every instinct screaming at me to run. There, under the Christmas tree, was a small, neatly wrapped box I hadn't put there. Its silver bow glinted in the dim light as the lid slowly lifted.

Inside was another wooden figure, identical to the first, but this one was even more distorted. Its grin stretched impossibly wide, splitting its head nearly in half, and its hands were held out, as if beckoning me closer.

The lights flickered. I turned, and there he was.

The Grinning Gifter.

He wasn't carved wood anymore. He was real—tall, gaunt, and impossibly thin, his crimson coat hanging off him like a shroud. His face was stretched into that same grotesque grin, his black eyes gleaming with malice.

He raised a long, bony finger to his lips. "Shhh," he whispered, his voice like dry leaves. Then he pointed to the second figure under the tree.

"Open it," he said, his grin never faltering. "Or I will."

I don't remember screaming. I don't remember running. All I remember is waking up in my room, drenched in sweat, the figures gone and the house eerily quiet. I thought it was over, a nightmare I couldn't explain.

Until Christmas morning.

There, under the tree, was a single wrapped box. No tag, no explanation. I didn't open it.

And now, every night, I hear him. Slow footsteps in the hall, the creak of the floorboards by my bed, and the soft, rasping sound of his laugh.

This Christmas, I'll open the box.

Because I know if I don't, **he will.**

6.The Christmas Lights Never Turn Off

Everyone in my town loved the Johnsons' Christmas lights. Their display was legendary—rows of glowing candy canes, reindeer with twinkling antlers, and strings of lights that draped their house like a shimmering blanket of holiday spirit. People came from miles away to see it, taking pictures and marveling at how much effort they put in every year.

But something about it always made me uneasy.

The lights weren't just beautiful; they were *too* perfect. They never flickered, never shorted out, no matter how bad the weather got. They glowed with a strange intensity, like they were alive. And they never turned off. Not even during the day.

"It's tradition," Mrs. Johnson would say with a cheerful laugh. "The lights stay on from December 1st to New Year's Day. It's our gift to the town!"

But last Christmas, the lights didn't turn off after New Year's Day. They didn't turn off *ever*.

At first, no one thought much of it. Maybe they forgot. Maybe they were just keeping the spirit alive a little longer. But weeks passed, and the lights stayed on, glowing brightly in the dead of winter. Snowstorms came and went, and still, the display shone as if powered by something far stronger than electricity.

People started to notice that the Johnsons weren't around. Their car never left the driveway. Their curtains were always drawn. When someone knocked on the door, there was no answer. But the lights burned on, brighter than ever.

By February, rumors began to spread. Some people said the Johnsons had gone on vacation and forgotten to turn the lights off. Others whispered about fires and electrical accidents. But no one really believed that. Deep down, everyone knew something was wrong.

I didn't want to get involved. But one night, as I walked home from work, I felt drawn to the Johnsons' house. It was late, the streets empty, and their house blazed like a beacon in the darkness.

I don't know why I went up to the porch. Maybe I wanted to prove to myself that there was nothing to be afraid of. Maybe I just needed to see for myself. Whatever the reason, I knocked on the door.

No answer.

I knocked again. The sound echoed, hollow and loud in the quiet night.

The door creaked open.

I hesitated, but curiosity—or maybe stupidity—pushed me inside. The house was cold. Too cold, like no one had been living there for weeks. The only light came from the glow of the decorations outside, casting eerie patterns on the walls.

"Hello?" I called out, my voice trembling. "Mr. Johnson? Mrs. Johnson?"

Silence.

I stepped further in, my breath fogging in the frigid air. The living room was empty, but there was something on the coffee table—a single Christmas ornament. It was a glass ball, clear and fragile, but inside it was a tiny, glowing light. I picked it up, and as I held it, I could swear I heard something—a faint, distant sound, like whispering.

The whispering grew louder, and then I realized: it wasn't coming from the ornament.

It was coming from the walls.

I dropped the ornament, and it shattered on the floor, the glowing light inside fizzling out. The whispering stopped, replaced by a low, mechanical hum. I turned to leave, but as I reached the door, the lights outside flared impossibly bright.

And then they started moving.

The strings of lights slithered across the walls like snakes, wrapping around the windows and doors, trapping me inside. I screamed, trying to pull the lights away, but they burned my hands like fire. The hum grew louder, vibrating through the floor, through my chest, until it was deafening.

And then I saw them.

The Johnsons.

They were standing in the doorway to the kitchen, their faces blank, their eyes glowing with the same unnatural light as the decorations. Their mouths moved, but no sound came out. They raised their hands, and the lights wrapped tighter around me, pulling me toward the living room.

Toward the tree.

The Christmas tree stood in the corner, its lights pulsing like a heartbeat. And at the base of the tree was something I hadn't noticed before—a pile of gifts, wrapped in shiny paper.

The boxes were moving.

I struggled against the lights, but they dragged me closer. One of the boxes burst open, and a hand—a human hand—reached out, clawing at the air. The other boxes started to shake, their lids splintering, more hands, more faces pressing against the wrapping paper.

The Johnsons didn't speak. They only smiled, their glowing eyes fixed on me.

I don't remember how I got out. I woke up hours later on my front lawn, my clothes singed and my hands covered in burns. When I looked back at the Johnsons' house, the lights were still on, brighter than ever.

The police didn't believe me. No one did. But people stopped going near the Johnsons' house after that. The lights are still on, even now, a year later.

And every night, I hear the hum. It's faint, but it's there, growing louder. I think they're waiting.

For me.

7.Frostclaw: The Beast of Christmas Eve

In the snowy town of Pine Hollow, we had a tradition that no one dared to break: never, *ever*, leave your doors or windows open on Christmas Eve. It wasn't about keeping the cold out—it was about keeping *him* out.

The legend of **Frostclaw** had been passed down for generations. They said he was once a man, a hunter who lived on the mountain. Desperate and starving during a brutal winter, he struck a deal with something ancient and evil. The creature promised him endless winter prey, but at a cost: his humanity.

Now, Frostclaw roams the snowy woods every Christmas Eve, his icy claws and jagged teeth seeking warmth and life to steal. He is drawn by open doors, flickering lights, and the scent of holiday feasts. And if he enters your home, he never leaves alone.

I never believed the stories. They sounded like something adults made up to keep kids from wandering out in the cold. But last Christmas Eve, I found out Frostclaw was real.

It was one of the coldest nights in years. My family had gathered for the usual festivities: hot cocoa, carols, and the crackling fire. But this year felt different. The wind howled louder than ever, rattling the windows and sending shivers down my spine.

Around 10 PM, my little sister Emily ran to the window. "It's snowing so much!" she said, her breath fogging up the glass.

"Close the curtain," my mom snapped, her voice sharp. "You know the rule."

Emily pouted but obeyed. I thought Mom was overreacting—after all, it was just a dumb story. But then I saw it.

A shadow.

It passed through the yard, barely visible against the swirling snow, but it was there—large and hulking, moving unnaturally fast. My heart skipped a beat as I pressed my face to the glass for a better look.

"Did you see that?" I whispered to Emily.

"See what?" she asked, her face pale.

Before I could answer, the power went out.

The room plunged into darkness, save for the faint glow of the dying fire. My dad cursed under his breath and grabbed a flashlight.

"It's probably the storm," he said, but his voice lacked conviction. "I'll check the breaker."

As he stepped into the basement, the wind outside grew louder, almost like it was alive. And then we heard it.

A scratching sound.

It was faint at first, but it grew louder, more frantic, coming from the back door.

"What is that?" Emily whispered, clutching my arm.

"Probably just a branch," I said, trying to sound brave. But deep down, I knew it wasn't.

The scratching stopped.

For a moment, everything was silent. Then, the back door handle rattled.

Mom grabbed the fire poker, her face pale. "Stay here," she hissed.

She crept toward the kitchen, but before she reached the door, the rattling stopped.

And then came the howl.

It wasn't a wolf or the wind—it was something else entirely. A deep, guttural sound that made the hairs on the back of my neck stand up.

"Dad!" I shouted, but there was no response.

The howl came again, closer this time.

I grabbed Emily's hand and ran to the basement, desperate to find Dad. But when we opened the door, he wasn't there. The flashlight he had taken was lying on the floor, flickering weakly. The air was colder than it should've been, frost creeping up the walls.

"Dad?" I called out, my voice shaking.

Something moved in the shadows.

A pair of glowing, ice-blue eyes stared back at us.

And then he stepped into the light.

Frostclaw.

He was enormous, his body covered in frostbitten fur that shimmered like ice. His claws were long and jagged, sharp enough to cut through steel. His face was a twisted snarl of jagged teeth and frozen flesh, his breath misting in the frigid air.

He took a step forward, his claws scraping against the floor.

"Run!" I screamed, pulling Emily back up the stairs.

We slammed the basement door shut and bolted it, but the scratching began almost immediately.

"He's going to get in!" Emily sobbed.

"Help me!" I shouted to Mom, but when I turned to the living room, she was gone. The front door was wide open, snow blowing inside.

"No," I whispered, realizing too late what had happened.

I grabbed the fire poker and stood in front of Emily, ready to fight. The scratching stopped, replaced by a deep, guttural laugh that echoed through the house.

"You left the door open," Frostclaw growled, his voice like cracking ice. "And now you're mine."

The door splintered, and the last thing I remember was his icy claws grabbing my arm, his freezing breath on my face.

I woke up in the snow, the sun rising over the frozen remains of my house. There was no sign of Frostclaw, no sign of Mom, Dad, or Emily.

But every Christmas Eve, I hear the scratching.

And I know he's coming back.

8.The Cemetery Claus

It was Christmas Eve, and the snow fell gently over Hollow Pines Cemetery. The wrought iron gates stood open, creaking softly in the wind. Most people avoided the place, especially at night, but not him.

Santa Claus.

No one ever thinks about the dead on Christmas, but maybe they should. After all, didn't they deserve to be remembered too? That's what Santa believed. And every year, after delivering presents to the living, he'd make one final stop at Hollow Pines.

The sleigh touched down silently between rows of ancient headstones. The reindeer, their breaths misting in the frosty air, shifted nervously. Even Rudolph's bright nose seemed dimmer in the cemetery's eerie stillness.

"Easy now," Santa said, his voice kind but firm. He grabbed his sack of gifts—smaller than the one he used for the living but just as full of good intentions—and began his rounds.

Santa moved through the cemetery with a reverence rarely seen. For each grave, he left a small token: a carved wooden toy, a knitted scarf, a sprig of holly tied with a red ribbon. They weren't much, but they were something—a reminder that the dead were not forgotten.

As he worked, a strange sensation began to settle over him. The air grew colder, the shadows longer. The snow, so peaceful when he arrived, now felt oppressive, muffling every sound except the crunch of his boots.

And then he heard it.

A voice. Faint at first, like a whisper carried on the wind.

"Santa..."

He froze, his gloved hand hovering over a headstone. The voice came again, stronger this time.

"Santa... stay with us..."

He turned, but the cemetery was empty. Only the shadows of the headstones and the skeletal trees greeted him.

"Who's there?" he called out, his usual jolly tone replaced with unease.

The voice didn't answer. Instead, the ground beneath him shifted. The snow seemed to melt away, revealing dark, frostbitten soil. A skeletal hand broke through the earth, followed by another, and then another.

The dead were rising.

Santa stumbled back, his sack of gifts falling to the ground. The graves around him cracked open like brittle ice, and figures began to emerge—emaciated bodies, their hollow eyes glowing faintly in the moonlight. They moved slowly, deliberately, their bony fingers reaching out for him.

"You've always come for us, Santa," one of them rasped, its voice a hollow echo. "But this year... stay."

He turned to run, but the path back to his sleigh was blocked by a wall of the dead. The reindeer screamed and reared, their hooves kicking at the snow. But Santa couldn't reach them.

"Let me go!" he shouted, his voice breaking. "I've done nothing but bring joy!"

The dead laughed—a cold, bone-chilling sound.

"Joy for the living," another said. "But what about us? You remember us only once a year. Stay, Santa. Let us have your joy."

Santa swung his sack wildly, the toys spilling out and scattering across the ground. The dead picked them up, their skeletal hands clutching the gifts with a disturbing reverence.

"Join us," they chanted, their voices growing louder, a cacophony of despair and longing.

Santa backed against a tall mausoleum, his breath coming in short, panicked gasps. The air was so cold now that frost formed on his beard.

"Please," he begged. "I still have work to do. There are children waiting for me."

The dead paused, their hollow eyes staring into his. For a moment, it seemed they might let him go.

Then one of them stepped forward—a child, no older than six, her form barely more than a skeleton wrapped in tattered cloth. She held out a tiny, frost-covered hand.

"Don't leave us, Santa," she whispered. "We're children too."

Santa's heart broke. He reached out to her, his gloved hand trembling, and when her icy fingers touched his, he felt it—a deep, piercing cold that spread through his body, freezing him from the inside out.

The dead closed in, their icy hands pulling him into the snow, into the earth. His laughter, once so jolly and full of life, faded into the howling wind.

By morning, the cemetery was silent again, the graves undisturbed. But if you visit Hollow Pines on Christmas Eve, you might see them—small gifts placed on the graves, and a figure in red moving among the tombstones, his eyes hollow, his once-jolly spirit now bound to the dead.

And if you listen closely, you might hear his voice, whispering softly from the shadows:

"Merry Christmas... to all... and to all... a good night..."

9.The Christmas Carnival

Every December, the Christmas Carnival arrived in our small town of Cedar Hollow like clockwork. Its bright lights and cheerful music transformed the frosty streets into a wonderland of holiday magic. Kids ran through the stalls, adults sipped mulled wine, and laughter filled the air.

But last year, the Carnival brought something else.

It was the final night, Christmas Eve, when the strangeness began. My friends and I were wandering through the carnival, our pockets stuffed with candy and our cheeks pink from the cold. We stopped at the prize booth, where a man in a too-wide smile stood behind the counter. His teeth gleamed unnaturally white, his eyes sharp like glass.

"What'll it be, kids?" he asked, his voice dripping with syrupy cheer.

We didn't notice the booth wasn't one we'd seen before. Or that his prizes—a strange assortment of dolls, carved figurines, and snow globes—seemed to shimmer oddly in the light.

"Five rings for a prize," he said, placing the hoops on the counter. "Try your luck!"

I tossed a ring, hitting the first bottle dead-on. The man's grin stretched wider, and for a moment, I thought I saw his teeth *shift*—becoming jagged and pointed. My stomach twisted, but I laughed it off. I tossed another ring, and another, each one landing perfectly.

"Looks like you're a natural," the man said, handing me my prize: a small, porcelain snow globe. Inside was a tiny carnival, the figures frozen in mid-celebration.

"Thanks," I said, clutching it tightly. But as I turned it over in my hands, I swore I saw the tiny figures move.

Later that night, back at home, the snow globe sat on my desk. I was staring at it, something about the tiny carnival drawing me in, when the snow inside began to swirl.

And then, the figures moved again.

One of them—a tiny man with a crooked top hat—turned his head toward me. His painted face cracked into a grin that looked eerily familiar.

"Come back to the Carnival," a voice whispered, low and raspy, as if it came from the depths of the snow globe.

I dropped it, the glass shattering on the floor. But instead of water and fake snow spilling out, a thick, black mist oozed from the shards. The room filled with the sound of laughter—not the warm, jolly kind, but cold, hollow laughter that sent shivers down my spine.

Out of the mist came the first creature: a hunched figure with clawed hands and glowing, yellow eyes. Its twisted face split into a grin, and it let out a guttural growl. More creatures followed—small, scaly gremlins with sharp teeth, ghouls with sunken faces and skeletal limbs, and shadowy figures that melted into the corners of the room.

They swarmed the house, tearing through walls and furniture, their raspy voices chanting:

"Come to the Carnival... Come to the Carnival..."

I ran outside, hoping it was just me. But the whole town was alive with chaos. Lights flickered, and the snowstorm had turned black, swirling with ash and embers. The Carnival rides were no longer joyful—they creaked and groaned, their shapes twisted and monstrous. The Ferris wheel spun uncontrollably, its seats dangling like severed limbs. The carousel played a warped, discordant tune as the horses reared and snapped at anyone who got too close.

In the center of it all stood the prize booth man, his human disguise gone. His skin was pale and cracked like porcelain, his too-wide grin revealing rows of razor-sharp teeth. Around him swarmed the creatures, his "prizes" brought to life.

"Welcome, Cedar Hollow!" he bellowed, his voice booming. "Your holiday cheer has been so *delicious*! But now, it's time for the main event!"

People screamed as the creatures dragged them toward the carnival. Some were pulled into the funhouse, where their cries were replaced by maniacal laughter. Others disappeared into the black mist surrounding the haunted roller coaster.

I ran, my heart pounding, but no matter where I went, the Carnival followed. The snow globe's voice echoed in my ears, promising, "You'll join us too."

By dawn, Cedar Hollow was gone.

The Carnival disappeared, leaving nothing but scorched earth and a few tattered decorations. The news called it a freak fire, but I knew the truth.

This year, the Christmas Carnival has appeared in another town, its lights glowing like a beacon. If you see it, don't go. Don't play the games, don't take the prizes, and whatever you do—don't look too closely at the snow globes.

Because once you do, the Carnival *always* comes back for you.

10.The Christmas Paradox

It was a cold Christmas Eve, and the streets of our small town glowed with the soft light of decorations. My family and I were gathered around the fire, the faint sound of carolers in the distance, when the knocking started.

Three sharp raps on the front door.

It was odd. No one was expected, and most people wouldn't brave the freezing night just for a visit. My dad got up to answer, and when he opened the door, there was a man standing there—a tall figure in a long, battered coat, with wild hair and an equally wild expression.

"Sorry to interrupt," he said, his voice cheerful but hurried. "But there's a bit of a situation outside, and I think you might want to come with me."

My dad looked at him, bewildered. "Who are you?"

"Oh, I'm the Doctor," he said, flashing a strange metal device with a glowing blue tip. "And we don't have much time."

Before we could respond, there was a loud, mechanical grinding noise from the street. The sound sent shivers down my spine. It wasn't the noise of any vehicle—it was deeper, more alien. The Doctor's expression darkened.

"They're here," he said simply.

We all ran to the window. At the far end of the street, something was moving through the fog—something massive. As it drew closer, I saw the unmistakable silhouette of a Christmas parade float. But this wasn't any normal float. The giant snowman at the front had glowing red eyes, and its carrot nose was spinning like a drill. The floats behind it were equally twisted—reindeer with jagged, metallic antlers, a sleigh bristling with spikes, and elves with robotic limbs marching in perfect unison.

"What *is* that?" I whispered.

"Ah," the Doctor said, scratching the back of his head. "Looks like a rogue group of Autons decided to get festive. Lovely timing, really."

"Autons?" my mom asked.

"Living plastic," the Doctor explained. "Controlled by the Nestene Consciousness. And right now, they seem to think Christmas is the perfect time for a takeover."

As he spoke, the snowman's drill-nose spun faster, and it charged toward a parked car, tearing through it like paper. The robotic elves swarmed behind, their hollow, featureless faces glowing faintly in the dark.

"We need to stop them!" the Doctor shouted, pulling a strange key from his pocket. He darted outside and ran to what I thought was an ordinary blue police box sitting on the curb.

"That's... not supposed to be there," my dad muttered.

The Doctor flung open the door, revealing an impossibly large, glowing room inside. "TARDIS," he said, grinning. "Bigger on the inside. Now come on!"

We didn't hesitate. Once inside, he flipped a series of switches on the console, and the room hummed to life. The sound of the marching Autons grew louder outside.

"Right, here's the plan," the Doctor said, grabbing a tangle of wires from beneath the console. "We need to disrupt their signal before they turn the whole town into a plastic nightmare. But the transmitter's probably hidden in the middle of their parade."

"Can't we just, I don't know, melt them?" my mom suggested.

"Oh, that'd only annoy them," the Doctor said. "We need precision."

With that, he handed me a strange device—a sleek, glowing rod that vibrated slightly in my hand. "You," he said, pointing to me. "Find the transmitter and point this at it. Simple!"

"Why me?" I stammered.

"Because you're brave," he said, smiling.

I wasn't sure if I believed him, but there wasn't time to argue. The Doctor opened the TARDIS door, and we stepped out into the chaos. The Autons had spread down the street, smashing windows and tearing through holiday decorations. The parade floats had merged into one massive, rolling monstrosity, the giant snowman perched on top like a grotesque king.

"Go!" the Doctor shouted. "I'll distract them!"

As he ran toward the snowman, waving his sonic screwdriver and shouting nonsense, I darted toward the parade float. The transmitter was obvious—a glowing orb embedded in the snowman's chest, pulsing with a sickly green light.

The plastic elves spotted me, their movements jerky and unnatural, and they charged. My heart raced as I aimed the device the Doctor had given me. A high-pitched whine filled the air, and the orb began to crackle. The snowman's red eyes flickered, and it let out a deep, guttural roar.

"Hurry!" the Doctor yelled, dodging a swipe from the snowman's drill.

I pressed a button on the device, and the orb shattered with a blinding flash of light. The Autons froze mid-step, their bodies collapsing into lifeless heaps of plastic. The snowman toppled forward, its jagged teeth inches from the Doctor before it crumbled into pieces.

The street was silent, save for the faint hum of the TARDIS.

"Well done!" the Doctor said, clapping me on the shoulder. "You just saved Christmas!"

As quickly as he'd arrived, he was gone. The TARDIS vanished with its signature grinding noise, leaving behind only the faint smell of ozone and the wreckage of the destroyed Autons.

To this day, I'm not sure if anyone else remembers what happened that night. The town cleaned up the mess, and people chalked it up to a freak accident.

But every Christmas Eve, when I hear the faint sound of the TARDIS in the distance, I smile. Somewhere out there, the Doctor is saving another Christmas.

11.The Ornament Keeper

Every year, my family had a tradition. On Christmas Eve, before going to bed, we'd hang the final ornament on the tree—a beautifully crafted glass bauble passed down for generations. It was always the last decoration, placed with care, a symbol of good fortune for the coming year.

This year, things were different.

We had just finished decorating the tree when my mom pulled out the ornament. It was strange—it didn't look like the one we'd used every year. Instead of the familiar red and gold, this one was a deep, smoky black with swirling silver veins.

"Where did that come from?" I asked, a shiver creeping up my spine.

"I found it in the attic," Mom said, turning it over in her hands. "Thought we could try something new this year."

My dad shrugged, and my little sister clapped her hands excitedly. "It's so pretty!" she said.

But I couldn't shake the feeling that something was wrong.

Reluctantly, we hung it on the tree. The lights from the tree seemed to dim slightly, their warm glow swallowed by the ornament's dark surface.

"Perfect," Mom said, stepping back to admire the tree.

That night, as I lay in bed, I couldn't sleep. The house was too quiet, the kind of silence that presses on your ears and makes you feel like you're not alone.

Then I heard it.

A faint, rhythmic sound—like glass tapping against glass.

I sat up, straining to hear. The sound was coming from the living room, where the tree stood. My heart pounded as I crept out of bed and down the hall.

The living room was bathed in the soft glow of the Christmas lights. At first, everything looked normal. But then I saw it.

The ornament.

It was spinning slowly on its branch, even though there was no draft in the room. Its dark surface shimmered as if something inside was moving.

And then it stopped.

The tapping sound grew louder, and I realized it wasn't coming from the ornament. It was coming from the window.

I turned, my breath catching in my throat.

A figure stood outside, its face hidden in the shadows. Its long, skeletal hand tapped against the glass, its nails clicking like icicles. I stumbled back, my heart racing, but the figure didn't move.

"Let me in," it whispered, its voice soft and cold, like the wind through bare trees.

I shook my head, unable to speak.

Its other hand reached out, pointing toward the tree. "You invited me," it said, and then its fingers curled into a fist.

The ornament cracked.

A spiderweb of fractures spread across its surface, and from inside came a deep, guttural growl. The tree lights flickered, and the room grew colder, frost creeping up the windows and walls.

The ornament shattered.

Something emerged from the shards—a dark, twisting shape that writhed and expanded, filling the room with shadows. The figure outside the window was gone, but its voice echoed in my ears.

"The Ornament Keeper thanks you for your gift."

The shadows coiled around the room, and I couldn't move, couldn't scream. My family rushed in, their faces pale as they saw the dark figure looming above the tree, its hollow eyes glowing faintly.

"Get out!" my dad shouted, but his voice was swallowed by the darkness.

The shadow laughed, a deep, resonant sound that shook the house. "You cannot undo what is given," it said. "I take what is mine."

And then it was gone.

The room was silent again, the tree standing untouched, but the ornament was nowhere to be seen. My family stood frozen, the horror of what we'd witnessed etched on their faces.

We didn't speak of it again.

But the next morning, under the tree, we found a new ornament. A deep, smoky black bauble with swirling silver veins.

We didn't hang it.

But no matter where we hid it, it always found its way back to the tree.

And now, every Christmas Eve, I hear the tapping on the window.

The Ornament Keeper is waiting.

12.The Christmas Rex

Every Christmas, my grandfather would tell us strange stories about his childhood growing up near Pine Ridge, a small town nestled against the mountains. One story always stuck with me—a tale about the **Christmas Rex**.

He claimed it happened when he was just a boy, during a blizzard so fierce it buried half the town in snow. That year, strange tracks appeared in the snow on Christmas morning—massive clawed footprints that no one could explain. Livestock went missing, homes were damaged, and people whispered about a monstrous beast roaming the woods.

"It's just an old legend," my dad would say whenever Grandpa told the story. "He's trying to scare you into behaving."

But last Christmas, I found out it wasn't just a story.

The blizzard hit on Christmas Eve, just like in Grandpa's tale. The wind howled like a living thing, shaking the house and rattling the windows. I stayed up late, staring out at the snow, half hoping to see the tracks Grandpa always talked about.

Around midnight, I heard it—a low, guttural roar that made the hairs on the back of my neck stand up. It wasn't the wind. It was deeper, louder, and filled with something primal.

I woke my little brother, Jake. "Did you hear that?" I whispered.

He groaned, rubbing his eyes. "What? It's just the wind."

But then we heard it again. Louder this time, and closer.

We crept to the window and looked outside. The snow glowed faintly in the moonlight, untouched except for a single set of tracks. They were massive, each footprint deep enough to swallow a car tire.

"What made that?" Jake whispered, his voice trembling.

"I don't know," I said. But deep down, I did.

The Christmas Rex.

The roar came again, and this time it shook the house. We ran to wake our parents, but they told us to go back to bed, blaming the storm for the noise.

"They won't believe us," Jake said. "We have to see it for ourselves."

I wasn't brave, but the curiosity—and fear—was too strong to ignore. We bundled up and snuck out the back door, following the tracks into the woods behind our house.

The snow was deep, and the wind bit at our faces, but we pressed on. The tracks led to a clearing, and in the center stood something out of a nightmare.

It was a dinosaur.

A towering tyrannosaurus rex, its body covered in a coat of frost and ice, steam rising from its massive jaws. Its scales shimmered like glass, reflecting the pale light of the moon. It was sniffing the air, its glowing eyes scanning the woods as it let out another earth-shaking roar.

In its claws was a sack. Not a sack of toys, but a torn bag of meat—raw and bloody.

"It's real," Jake whispered, his voice filled with awe and terror.

The beast turned, its massive head snapping in our direction. For a moment, I thought it was going to charge, but then something even stranger happened.

It dropped the sack and leaned down, its glowing eyes fixed on us. From its massive jaws came a low, almost gentle growl, like it was waiting for something.

Jake reached into his pocket and pulled out a candy cane he'd been saving from earlier. Slowly, he held it out.

The Christmas Rex sniffed the air, then tilted its head. It reached out with one claw, delicately plucking the candy cane from Jake's hand.

For a moment, it stood there, crunching the candy cane between its massive teeth. Then it turned and lumbered back into the woods, leaving the sack of meat behind.

We ran back to the house, hearts pounding. The tracks were gone by morning, buried in the fresh snow.

No one believed us, of course. But every Christmas Eve, we leave out a candy cane in the woods, just in case.

And every year, it's gone by morning.

13.The Christmas Cat Curse

It started three Christmases ago, when my grandmother passed away. She'd lived alone in her little cottage at the edge of town, surrounded by her beloved cats. There were dozens of them, strays she'd taken in over the years, and she loved them more than anything else in the world.

When we cleaned out her house after the funeral, the cats wouldn't leave. They sat on the porch, in the yard, their glowing eyes watching us silently as we packed her things. We thought they'd scatter eventually, but they didn't. Every time we visited the property, they were there, like they were waiting for something.

We didn't think much of it. Not until Christmas Eve.

That year, the cats showed up at *our* house. At first, it was just one or two on the porch, but by midnight, there were dozens. They sat in perfect stillness, their eyes reflecting the twinkling Christmas lights.

"What do they want?" my mom asked, her voice shaking.

"They're just strays," my dad said, though he sounded unsure. "They'll go away."

But they didn't.

That night, I woke up to the sound of scratching at my bedroom window. I opened the curtains and found one of the cats staring at me, its green eyes wide and unblinking. It wasn't scratching at the glass—it was tapping, like it was trying to get in.

I shut the curtains and tried to go back to sleep, but the tapping didn't stop.

By morning, the cats were gone, leaving strange tracks in the snow that didn't look like paw prints. They were too big, too elongated, almost... human.

The next year, it happened again. Christmas Eve, the cats returned, but this time, there were more. They surrounded the house, their glowing eyes watching from every window.

And that night, the tapping wasn't just at my window. It was at every window, every door.

I didn't sleep at all.

By Christmas morning, they were gone, but something was left behind. On the porch was a small, bloodied gift box. Inside was a tuft of fur and something else—a tooth. A human tooth.

This year, I begged my parents to spend Christmas somewhere else. Anywhere but home. They didn't believe me about the cats, but they agreed just to humor me.

On Christmas Eve, we stayed in a cozy cabin in the mountains, far from the house and the haunting cats. For the first time in years, I felt safe.

But that night, as the clock struck midnight, I heard it.

The tapping.

I looked out the window, and there they were. The cats. Hundreds of them, their glowing eyes fixed on the cabin. They were closer this time, pressed against the glass, their bodies too still, their eyes too intelligent.

And then I heard the whispering.

It was faint at first, like the wind, but it grew louder, words I couldn't understand. And through the whispering came a single, clear voice—a woman's voice, cold and sharp as ice.

"You didn't keep your promise."

My blood ran cold. It was my grandmother's voice.

"What promise?" I whispered back, my breath fogging the glass.

The cats moved in unison, parting to reveal something behind them—a shadowy figure, tall and thin, with glowing eyes like theirs. It stepped closer, its face obscured, and reached out a long, clawed hand toward the window.

I screamed, and the glass shattered.

When I woke up, it was Christmas morning. My parents found me outside the cabin, curled up in the snow, surrounded by paw prints that weren't quite paw prints.

We're back home now, but I know it's not over. Every night since Christmas, I've heard the tapping, and every morning, I find a gift on the porch—small boxes filled with fur, bones, and teeth.

The cats are waiting for something.
And I think this year, they'll come inside.

14.The Elves on the Shelf

Everyone knows about Elf on the Shelf. It's supposed to be cute—a fun little Christmas tradition where the elf "watches" you to make sure you're being good. But last Christmas, I found out there's more to it than anyone lets on.

It started when my little brother, Tommy, begged for an elf. He'd seen the commercials, the books, and his friends at school had all talked about how magical their elves were. My mom finally caved and bought one the day after Thanksgiving.

It looked innocent enough when we unboxed it. The elf had a red suit, a frozen smile, and those wide, unblinking eyes that seemed just a little too lifelike. Tommy named it Jingles, and every night, he'd whisper to it, telling it about his day and his Christmas wishes.

At first, nothing seemed unusual. Jingles would appear in a new spot every morning—on the mantel, hanging from the tree, even in the fridge once. Tommy thought it was hilarious. I thought it was Mom moving it around.

But then, strange things started happening.

One morning, we found Jingles sitting on the kitchen counter next to a broken plate. Mom swore she hadn't moved him, and Tommy insisted he hadn't either. Then, ornaments started falling off the tree, even though no one was near it. A week later, our dog, Max, refused to go near the living room, growling at the elf whenever he saw it.

"It's just a doll," Mom said when I brought it up. But I could tell she was starting to feel uneasy too.

The night before Christmas Eve, I decided to put the whole thing to rest. While Tommy was asleep, I grabbed Jingles and stuffed him back into his box, planning to hide it in the attic.

But when I opened the box the next morning, it was empty.

Jingles was back on the mantel, staring at me with that fixed, unnerving grin. But something was different. His hands were clasped in front of him, holding a tiny piece of paper. I unfolded it, my hands shaking, and read the single word written in jagged, childish handwriting:

"Naughty."

That night, I stayed awake, determined to catch whoever was moving the elf. The house was silent, the only light coming from the Christmas tree. Midnight came and went, and nothing happened. I started to drift off, thinking maybe I was overreacting.

Then I heard the sound.

A faint, scuttling noise, like tiny feet on the hardwood floor.

I froze, my heart pounding. The sound grew louder, moving closer to my room. Slowly, I turned my head toward the door.

Jingles was there, standing in the doorway.

But he wasn't a doll anymore.

He moved, his head tilting unnaturally as he stared at me with those cold, glassy eyes. His grin had stretched wider, revealing sharp, needle-like teeth.

"You're awake," he said, his voice high-pitched and raspy.

I couldn't move, couldn't scream. He climbed onto my bed, his tiny hands gripping the blanket as he crawled closer.

"You've been naughty," he whispered. "And naughty children get a visit from the others."

"The others?" I managed to choke out.

He smiled wider. "The workshop doesn't just make toys."

Before I could react, the room filled with more of the scuttling sounds. From the shadows, they emerged—other elves, dozens of them, their faces twisted into sinister grins, their hands claw-like and twitching. They surrounded the bed, their laughter low and menacing.

Jingles leaned in close, his cold breath on my face. "Don't worry," he said. "We'll take you somewhere *special*."

I screamed as they grabbed me, their tiny hands impossibly strong. The last thing I remember was the sound of jingling bells and the world going dark.

When I woke up, it was Christmas morning. I was back in my bed, but everything felt wrong. My family acted like nothing had happened, but Jingles was gone. The mantel was empty, and when I asked about him, my mom just gave me a confused look.

"What elf?" she said. "We never had one."

But I remember. And sometimes, late at night, I hear the faint sound of bells, and the scuttling of tiny feet just outside my door.

I know they're still watching. And I know they'll come back.

Because once the elves mark you as naughty, they never let you go.

15.The Night of Crimson Lights

Christmas Eve in Hollow Creek wasn't exactly festive. Our tiny town had more dive bars than holiday spirit, and the only thing glowing brighter than the string lights on Main Street was the neon "Girls Girls Girls" sign outside a place called **The Velvet Fang**.

It wasn't my usual scene, but my buddy Eric insisted we check it out. "Come on, it's Christmas Eve," he said, grinning. "Let's get a drink and see some *entertainment*."

The place was packed with the usual crowd—shifty-eyed regulars nursing cheap beer, holiday refugees looking for distraction, and a few guys already too drunk to stand. The air was heavy with cigarette smoke and cheap cologne, the dim lights casting shadows that seemed to stretch too far.

But then, the dancers came out, and everything changed.

The music started—a low, pulsing beat that made the walls vibrate. Three women strutted onto the stage, each more mesmerizing than the last. They wore crimson lingerie that glimmered in the dim light, their skin pale as snow. But it wasn't their beauty that caught my attention—it was their eyes. They glowed faintly, like embers, and when they smiled, I swore I saw something sharp behind their ruby-red lips.

"Dude, they're incredible," Eric whispered, his eyes glued to the stage.

I nodded, but something about them put me on edge. The way they moved wasn't natural—too fluid, too precise, like they were gliding instead of walking. And their gazes weren't just seductive; they were predatory.

The leader, a tall woman with jet-black hair and a serpentine grace, locked eyes with me. My throat tightened as she leaned into the microphone, her voice dripping with an accent I couldn't place.

"Merry Christmas, boys," she purred. "We have a special gift for you tonight. Stay late, and you'll see the real show."

The crowd cheered, but I felt a chill crawl up my spine.

As the night went on, the dancers grew more... aggressive. Their routines were hypnotic, almost otherworldly, and the men in the crowd couldn't look away. One by one, guys started disappearing—heading toward the back rooms with the dancers, never to return.

When Eric's name was called, he grinned and slapped me on the back. "Wish me luck, man."

"Wait," I said, grabbing his arm. "Something's not right."

"Don't be such a buzzkill," he laughed, shrugging me off.

I watched him follow the black-haired dancer through a velvet curtain, my stomach churning. Minutes passed. Then an hour. Eric didn't come back.

I decided to investigate.

The curtain led to a dark hallway, the music from the stage fading into an ominous hum. The air grew colder the further I went, and the walls seemed to close in around me. At the end of the hall was a heavy wooden door, slightly ajar.

Inside was something out of a nightmare.

Eric was slumped in a chair, his head tilted back, his neck pale and punctured. Standing over him was the black-haired dancer, her mouth smeared with blood. Two other dancers stood nearby, their fangs glistening as they drained another unlucky patron.

"You shouldn't be here," the black-haired woman said, her glowing eyes locking onto mine.

I stumbled back, but before I could run, she was in front of me, moving faster than I thought possible. Her cold hand gripped my wrist like a vise.

"Don't worry," she whispered, her breath cold against my neck. "You'll feel the Christmas spirit soon enough."

I shoved her away and ran, adrenaline pushing me faster than I thought possible. The hallway twisted and turned, the exit always seeming just out of reach. Behind me, I heard the dancers laughing—a cold, chilling sound that echoed through the halls.

I burst back into the main room, expecting chaos, but the bar was empty. No patrons, no bartenders, no music. The stage was dark, and the air was thick with the metallic scent of blood.

Only the neon sign outside remained, its flickering light casting eerie shadows across the room.

I didn't stop running until I was home.

The next morning, the Velvet Fang was gone. The building stood empty, as if it had never been there at all. Eric's disappearance was chalked up to a holiday getaway, but I knew the truth.

Sometimes, late at night, I see the glow of red lights in the distance. And when Christmas Eve rolls around, I hear whispers—soft, seductive voices calling my name, promising a night I'll never forget.

I never go back.

But the Velvet Fang is out there, waiting for new prey. If you see it, if you hear the music and see the crimson lights, don't go inside.

Because their gift is your blood, and the price is your soul.

16.The Howling Yule

The village of Frosthaven was famous for its Christmas traditions. Every year, the townsfolk would gather in the snowy square, stringing up lights, singing carols, and drinking mulled cider beneath the towering Yule tree. It was a picture-perfect holiday scene.

Except for one rule: **never stay out after the bells.**

The warning had been passed down for generations, as much a part of Christmas as the stockings and wreaths. Every Christmas Eve at precisely 10 PM, the church bells would ring twelve times, echoing through the frosty air. When they did, the streets emptied, doors were bolted, and shutters drawn tight.

No one ever explained why.

This Christmas Eve, I learned the reason.

My family had moved to Frosthaven a few months earlier, eager for a quiet holiday season. The townsfolk were friendly but tight-lipped about their strange tradition. When I asked what happened after the bells, they'd just shake their heads.

"Just stay inside," the innkeeper said, her voice low. "It's safer that way."

I was curious, of course. Too curious.

That night, as the festivities wound down and people started retreating to their homes, I lingered in the square. The Yule tree's lights glowed softly, and the snow fell in lazy, shimmering flakes. It felt magical, and I wasn't ready to leave.

Then the bells rang.

The sound was deep and mournful, louder than I expected. It seemed to echo through my chest, vibrating the very air. The square, once lively and bustling, emptied in seconds. People vanished into their homes, slamming doors and pulling curtains tight.

I was alone.

At first, nothing happened. The bells faded, leaving an eerie silence in their wake. The snow muffled every sound, and the lights of the Yule tree cast long shadows across the square.

And then I heard it.

A low, guttural growl.

I froze, my breath hanging in the air. The growl came again, closer this time, and then a sound that made my blood run cold: a long, bone-chilling howl that echoed through the night.

I turned toward the sound and saw them.

Eyes. Glowing yellow eyes, peering out from the shadows of the forest at the edge of town. One pair, then two, then dozens. The growling grew louder, blending with the crunch of snow as something massive moved through the trees.

The first one stepped into the light.

It was a wolf—but not like any wolf I'd ever seen. It was huge, its fur dark and matted with patches of frost. Its jaws were too long, its teeth jagged and glistening. And its eyes weren't just animal—they were intelligent. Hungry.

More followed, their hulking forms emerging from the woods like shadows come to life. They moved on two legs, their clawed hands dragging across the ground as they sniffed the air.

I turned to run, but my foot slipped on the icy cobblestones, sending me sprawling to the ground. The nearest wolf snapped its head toward me, its lips pulling back in a snarl.

The pack moved as one, their claws scraping against the stone as they closed in.

"Over here!" a voice hissed.

I looked up to see a man standing in the doorway of a nearby shop, frantically waving me inside. I scrambled to my feet and darted toward him, the wolves' snarls growing louder behind me.

The man slammed the door shut the moment I was inside, bolting it with shaking hands. He gestured for me to follow him deeper into the shop, away from the windows.

"You're lucky," he said, his voice low. "Most don't make it this far."

"What are those things?" I asked, my heart racing.

He glanced toward the window, where shadows moved against the frosted glass. "They're the Yule Wolves," he said. "They come every Christmas Eve to hunt."

"Why doesn't anyone stop them? Call for help?"

He laughed bitterly. "You can't stop them. They're not just wolves—they're cursed. Every full moon of December, they come down from the mountains, drawn by the lights, the sounds, the smells. We survive by staying out of their way."

Outside, the growling grew louder, followed by the sound of claws scratching against the door. I held my breath as something massive thudded against the wood.

"They can smell you," the man whispered. "Once they catch your scent, they don't stop."

The scratching turned to pounding, the door buckling under the weight of their attacks. The man grabbed an old rifle from behind the counter, his hands trembling as he loaded it.

"Stay behind me," he said.

The door shattered, and the first wolf lunged inside, its jaws snapping. The man fired, the shot echoing through the small shop, but it only staggered the beast. More poured in, their claws tearing through shelves and displays.

I grabbed a broken piece of wood from the wreckage and swung it wildly, the splintered edge catching one wolf across the face. It yelped, but another was already behind it, its claws swiping at my leg.

The man shouted something, but I didn't hear it. The last thing I saw was the Yule tree outside, its lights flickering in the darkness as the wolves dragged me to the ground.

When I woke up, it was Christmas morning. The square was pristine, the snow untouched. There was no sign of the wolves or the destruction they'd caused.

But when I looked down at my leg, I saw it: a deep, jagged bite.

The wound hasn't healed.
And sometimes, when the moon is full, I feel the pull of the forest.
Next Christmas, I'll be with them. **Hunting.**

17. The Silent Night Horde

It was supposed to be a quiet Christmas. Snow fell softly on the streets of Willow Pines, the kind of picturesque scene you'd find on a holiday postcard. My family and I were gathered around the fire, sipping cocoa and watching *It's a Wonderful Life* when the emergency broadcast interrupted.

The screen flickered to static, then a grim-faced man in a rumpled suit appeared. "Stay indoors," he said, his voice shaky. "Lock your doors and windows. Do not engage with anyone showing unusual behavior."

"What's this?" my dad muttered, grabbing the remote to change the channel. But it was the same on every station. The man's voice grew more frantic.

"Reports are coming in of widespread violence. Symptoms include pale skin, vacant stares, and—" The feed cut out, replaced by a high-pitched whine.

And then we heard the first scream.

It came from down the street, piercing the cold night air. My dad rushed to the window and pulled back the curtain. Outside, the snow was no longer pristine. It was streaked with red.

Figures stumbled through the storm, their movements jerky and unnatural. They weren't dressed for the cold—no coats, no hats—just tattered clothes that hung off their skeletal frames. Their faces were pale, their mouths smeared with something dark. Blood.

"What the hell is going on?" my mom whispered, clutching my little sister, Emma.

Then came the banging.

Something—or someone—was pounding on our front door.

"Help me!" a voice cried, muffled by the thick wood.

My dad hesitated, but before he could unlock the door, I grabbed his arm. "Wait," I said. "What if it's... one of them?"

The banging stopped, replaced by a low growl. Then a second. And a third.

"They're surrounding the house," I whispered, my stomach churning.

From the window, I saw more of them approaching. Their eyes were hollow, their jaws slack, and their hands dragged through the snow, leaving deep, claw-like grooves. One of them—a woman in a torn Christmas sweater—stopped and looked directly at me. Her head tilted, and then she opened her mouth and let out a guttural screech that sent chills down my spine.

The others responded instantly, their movements becoming faster, more coordinated. They clawed at the windows, their nails scraping against the glass, leaving smears of blood and frost.

"Get upstairs!" my dad yelled, grabbing a fire poker.

We barricaded ourselves in the attic, the sound of breaking glass and splintering wood echoing through the house. Emma clung to me, tears streaming down her face.

"What do they want?" she whispered.

"They're zombies," I said, though the word felt ridiculous in my mouth. "They want us."

The sounds grew louder as they swarmed the house, their snarls filling the air. The attic door rattled, and I could see their pale, clawed hands reaching through the gaps in the wood.

Then everything went silent.

For a moment, all I could hear was the sound of my own breathing. My dad held the fire poker tightly, his knuckles white.

And then the singing started.

It was faint at first, but unmistakable—a warped, haunting rendition of *Silent Night*. The sound grew louder, the voices blending together in a discordant harmony. It came from the horde, their rotting mouths forming the words even as blood dripped from their lips.

"Silent night... holy night..."

"What the hell is this?" my dad whispered.

The singing stopped abruptly, replaced by heavy thuds on the roof. They were climbing. One of them broke through a weak spot, its skeletal face appearing through the hole, teeth snapping. My dad swung the poker, knocking it back, but more hands burst through, clawing and tearing.

"We're not going to make it!" my mom screamed.

I grabbed Emma and held her close, my heart racing as the attic filled with snow and blood and the stench of decay.

And then I heard it—a different sound. A deep, resonant bell tolling in the distance. The zombies froze, their heads snapping toward the sound.

The bell tolled again, and they began to retreat, their movements stiff and jerky. One by one, they disappeared into the storm, leaving our house in ruins.

"What just happened?" I whispered, my voice shaking.

None of us had an answer. We stayed in the attic until dawn, too scared to move. When the sun rose, the snow was untouched, as if the horde had never been there.

But the next night, I saw them again, standing in the distance, their hollow eyes fixed on our house.

They're waiting for Christmas to come again.

And this time, I don't think they'll stop.

18. Table for the Slaughter

Every year, my family celebrated Christmas at home. But last year, my dad decided to change things up. He booked us a table at a new restaurant called **"The Holly Hearth."** It had just opened in a secluded area outside of town, and everyone was raving about their "unforgettable Christmas Eve dinner."

We arrived just after sunset. The building looked like something out of a snow globe—quaint and picturesque, with twinkling lights and wreaths on every window. Inside, the smell of roasted meat and spiced cider filled the air, and a warm fire crackled in the stone hearth.

A hostess dressed as Mrs. Claus greeted us with a wide smile. "Welcome to The Holly Hearth," she said. "We're so glad you chose to spend your holiday with us."

Her teeth seemed too perfect, too sharp, but I chalked it up to my imagination.

The dining room was cozy, with just a few other families seated around long, festively decorated tables. A group of servers dressed as elves brought out steaming plates of food, their movements precise and coordinated. The whole place had an eerie sense of perfection, like it had been staged for a Christmas card.

We were seated near the fire, and the "elves" quickly served us complimentary cider. It was warm and sweet, but there was an odd metallic aftertaste I couldn't place. My little brother, Timmy, didn't seem to notice. He was already on his second glass.

"They really went all out, huh?" Dad said, looking around.

Mom nodded, but she seemed distracted, her eyes lingering on the servers. "Doesn't something feel... off?" she whispered to me.

Before I could answer, the lights dimmed, and the hostess reappeared. This time, she carried a small silver bell.

"Ladies and gentlemen," she said, her voice melodic but cold. "Thank you for joining us tonight. Before we begin the main course, we have a little tradition here at The Holly Hearth. A toast to the season!"

The other families raised their glasses, so we did too, though something about the moment made my skin crawl.

"To joy," the hostess said.

"To giving," the diners echoed.

"To the feast," she finished, her smile widening.

As we drank, I noticed something strange. The families at the other tables looked... dazed. Their movements were sluggish, their eyes unfocused. Even Timmy, who was usually full of energy, seemed to sag in his chair.

"Are you okay?" I whispered, nudging him. He didn't respond.

I turned to Mom, but before I could speak, the hostess clapped her hands. The servers moved in unison, locking the doors and pulling heavy curtains over the windows.

"What's going on?" Dad asked, standing up.

The hostess smiled. "Oh, don't worry. You're the *guests of honor.*"

The room fell silent, except for the sound of the fire crackling. The other families weren't moving anymore. They sat slumped in their chairs, their faces slack, their glasses still clutched in their hands.

And then the smell hit me. Not the warm, savory aroma of roasted meat, but something sharp and metallic—blood.

The elves began clearing the tables, but not the dishes. They dragged the families from their chairs, their lifeless bodies leaving smears of red across the polished wood floors.

"Oh my God!" Mom screamed, grabbing Timmy. "We have to get out of here!"

Dad charged at one of the servers, but the elf moved with inhuman speed, knocking him to the ground with a single blow.

"You don't understand," the hostess said, her voice calm. "This isn't just a restaurant. It's a tradition. A *sacrifice*."

"What are you talking about?" I shouted, my voice shaking.

"The Holly Hearth is special," she said. "Every Christmas, we prepare a feast for those who deserve it most. And tonight, *you* are the feast."

The servers advanced, their smiles now sharp and menacing. Their elf costumes were smeared with blood, and their eyes gleamed with hunger.

We fought. We tried to run. But the cider had done something to us. My legs felt like lead, my head spinning as the room blurred around me.

The last thing I saw was Timmy being dragged toward the kitchen, his small voice crying out for help.

I woke up to the sound of laughter and clinking glasses.

I was on a silver platter, surrounded by garnishes of holly and rosemary. My hands and feet were bound, my skin coated in a sticky glaze. The other families were laid out on long tables, their eyes wide and glassy.

The diners were back, but they weren't human anymore. Their faces were elongated, their teeth sharp and glistening. They dug into the feast with wild abandon, their claws tearing into the meat.

Somewhere in the distance, I heard the hostess's voice.

"Merry Christmas," she said, her laugh echoing through the room. "And to all, a good bite."

19. The Goblins' Feast and the Wendigo's Curse

In the snowy woods beyond our small town, the locals told stories of the **Goblins' Feast**—a gathering of strange, shadowy creatures that happened every Christmas Eve. They whispered about lights flickering in the forest, about goblins sneaking into homes to steal food, toys, and even children.

But those were just stories. Or so I thought.

Last Christmas, my cousins and I decided to investigate the legend. It started as a joke, a way to escape the boring family dinner. Armed with flashlights and our phones, we trudged into the woods, the snow crunching beneath our boots.

We followed a trail that seemed oddly deliberate—small footprints, too large for a child yet too small for a man, winding through the trees. After about an hour, the forest grew unnaturally quiet. The air felt heavy, and the shadows stretched longer than they should.

Then we saw it.

A clearing bathed in an eerie green glow. Strange, hunched figures scurried around a massive bonfire, their shapes distorted by the flickering flames. They were goblins—short, gnarled creatures with spindly limbs, pointed ears, and glowing red eyes.

And they were feasting.

On a massive stone table lay the remains of something—something that had been alive. The goblins tore into it with jagged teeth, their high-pitched laughter echoing through the forest. Around the fire, piles of toys and stolen Christmas decorations glittered like macabre trophies.

"Let's get out of here," my cousin Daniel whispered, his voice trembling.

But before we could move, one of the goblins sniffed the air and turned toward us. Its eyes locked onto mine, and it grinned, revealing rows of sharp, yellowed teeth.

"Guests!" it screeched. The others froze, their heads snapping in our direction.

We ran.

The goblins shrieked, their clawed feet scratching against the snow as they chased us through the trees. My heart pounded, my breath coming in ragged gasps. I could hear their laughter growing louder, closer.

Then the howling started.

It wasn't the goblins. This was deeper, more primal—a sound that seemed to shake the earth itself. The goblins stopped in their tracks, their eyes wide with fear.

"Wendigo," one of them hissed, its voice barely audible.

The trees around us groaned and creaked, their branches twisting as something massive approached. Through the shadows, I saw it—a towering figure, gaunt and skeletal, its eyes burning like embers in a hollow, skull-like face. Antlers crowned its head, and its long, clawed hands scraped against the ground as it moved.

The Wendigo.

The goblins scattered, their shrieks fading into the distance. But the Wendigo wasn't interested in them. It turned its gaze to us.

"You've trespassed," it said, its voice a guttural growl that echoed in my bones.

"We're sorry!" I stammered, backing away.

The Wendigo stepped closer, its skeletal frame towering over me. "Sorry will not save you," it said. "You've seen the Feast. You've seen what should remain hidden."

It raised one clawed hand, and the air grew colder, the snow beneath us turning to ice. My cousins and I tried to run, but the Wendigo's gaze pinned us in place.

The Wendigo's voice deepened, each word vibrating through my skull. "You will carry my curse, and through you, the Feast will spread."

I felt the air shift, an invisible force wrapping around me like freezing chains. My body burned with icy pain, and my vision blurred. Daniel screamed, but his voice cut off as the Wendigo's claws brushed against his forehead, leaving a blackened mark that shimmered faintly in the moonlight.

"Run," the Wendigo growled. "Spread the Feast, or the hunger will claim you."

Then it vanished, dissolving into the shadows as if it had never been there. The forest fell silent again, except for the ragged sound of our breathing. We didn't wait to figure out what had just happened. We ran, stumbling through the snow, our limbs numb from fear and cold.

When we finally reached home, the house was dark and empty. My parents and cousins' families were gone, the table still set for dinner, plates untouched. On the front door was a single, clawed scratch mark.

"They were taken," Daniel whispered, his voice shaking. "The goblins must've…"

"We have to get help," I said, but I knew it was hopeless. Who would believe us?

That night, we locked every door and window, but sleep didn't come. The blackened mark on Daniel's forehead glowed faintly in the darkness, and no matter how many blankets I piled on, I couldn't shake the cold.

Then the hunger started.

At first, it was a faint gnawing sensation, but it grew, spreading through my stomach and chest like fire. I raided the fridge, devouring everything in sight, but nothing satisfied the hunger. Daniel was the same, tearing into leftover turkey with trembling hands, his eyes wide and desperate.

As the days passed, the hunger grew worse. We couldn't leave the house, couldn't explain what was happening. And then, on the fifth day after Christmas, we heard the voices.

The goblins were back.

We saw them through the windows, circling the house, their red eyes glowing in the darkness. They chanted in a language I didn't understand, their clawed hands scraping against the walls.

And then, just like before, the howling began.

The Wendigo returned, its skeletal form emerging from the shadows. But this time, it didn't speak. It just stared at us through the window, its burning eyes filled with a terrible hunger that mirrored our own.

"We're going to become like them," Daniel whispered, his voice barely audible. "The goblins... the Wendigo... it's making us like them."

I didn't want to believe it, but deep down, I knew he was right. The hunger wasn't just physical. It was changing us, twisting us into something else. My reflection in the window looked wrong—my skin too pale, my teeth too sharp.

That night, the goblins entered the house.

We didn't fight. We didn't run. We joined them, their laughter echoing in our ears as the Wendigo watched from the shadows. The Feast had claimed us, and now we were part of it.

Every Christmas since, the hunger drives us back to the woods. We light the bonfire, we lay the feast, and we wait. For the lights. For the songs. For new trespassers to join us.

If you hear the howling in the woods on Christmas Eve, turn back. Do not follow the trail. Do not look for the Feast. Because if you see it, you'll never leave.

You'll join the goblins at the table, and the Wendigo will be watching, waiting, as the hunger takes you too.

20. The Ink of Christmas Night

Harold Fenwick was a modestly successful horror author, known for his knack for twisting the mundane into the macabre. But his sales had been dwindling, and his publisher demanded something fresh—something terrifying.

"Christmas horror," his editor had said. "Twisted holiday stories are trending. Write me a killer collection by Christmas, and I'll make sure it flies off the shelves."

Desperate to keep his career alive, Harold locked himself in his study, fueled by coffee and resentment. He tapped away at his keyboard, spinning tales of murderous elves, haunted ornaments, and malevolent Christmas trees. His mind was a whirlwind of dark creativity, and by the time Christmas Eve rolled around, his manuscript, *Tales of Christmas Night*, was complete.

That evening, as snow fell gently outside his window, Harold leaned back in his chair, exhausted but satisfied. The fire crackled in the hearth, and his house was eerily quiet—a perfect backdrop for horror.

That's when he heard it.

A faint rustling, like paper being crumpled. At first, he thought it was his imagination, but the sound grew louder, coming from his desk. His manuscript sat where he had left it, the pages neatly stacked. But something about it felt... wrong.

The pages fluttered, though there was no draft. A deep, guttural laugh echoed through the room, and Harold's heart raced. Slowly, he reached for the manuscript, but the moment his fingers touched the pages, the ink began to bleed.

Dark, inky tendrils seeped from the words, curling into the air like smoke. They twisted and writhed, forming shapes—shapes Harold recognized all too well.

The first to emerge was a figure from his opening story, *The Grinning Elf*. It was grotesque, with jagged teeth and hollow eyes, its tiny frame twitching unnaturally. It scuttled across the desk, its movements jerky and insect-like.

Harold stumbled back, his breath catching in his throat. "This isn't real," he whispered. "It's not real."

But it was.

From the shadows of the room, a massive Christmas tree emerged, its branches sharp as blades, its ornaments glowing with malevolent light. The tree creaked and groaned, its roots dragging across the floor as it moved toward him.

"No," Harold muttered, his voice trembling. "This can't be happening."

The ink bled faster, pooling on the floor and spreading across the room. One by one, his creations crawled, slithered, and stumbled into existence. The Gingerbread Golem, with its cracked, icing-covered body and razor-sharp candy cane claws. The Singing Ornaments, their voices warped and discordant as they sang *Silent Night* in a haunting, otherworldly tone.

"Why?" Harold screamed, backing against the wall. "Why is this happening?"

A voice, low and cold, answered from the shadows. "You gave us life, Harold. You brought us into existence."

The voice belonged to a figure draped in black robes, its face obscured by a veil of shadow. Harold recognized it immediately—it was *The Inkweaver*, the antagonist from his final story, a being that turned stories into nightmares.

"I-I didn't mean to," Harold stammered. "It was just fiction."

The Inkweaver tilted its head, its voice dripping with mockery. "Your words gave us form. Your fears gave us power. And now, we are free."

The creatures closed in, their eyes gleaming with malice. The Grinning Elf leapt onto Harold's chest, its claws digging into his flesh. The Singing Ornaments wrapped their glowing cords around his throat, their haunting song growing louder as he struggled.

The Inkweaver stood motionless, watching as Harold's creations tore into him. "Merry Christmas, Harold," it said, its voice echoing through the room. "Your stories will live forever."

When the townsfolk found Harold's house the next day, they thought it was abandoned. The doors were locked, the windows frosted over. But inside, his study was in ruins. Pages of his manuscript were scattered everywhere, smeared with ink and something darker.

On the desk, written in Harold's handwriting, was a single sentence: **"The best stories are the ones that come to life."**

No one ever published *Tales of Christmas Night*. But sometimes, on Christmas Eve, people in the town claim to see strange figures—grinning elves, murderous trees, and shadowy ornaments—lurking in the darkness.

And if you listen closely, you might hear their voices, singing softly: "Silent night, deadly night…"

21. The Christmas Cake

It started as a holiday baking tradition in our small town of Everpine. Every year, the town held a Christmas Cake contest, where families and bakeries would compete to make the most extravagant and delicious cake. This year, my mom was determined to win.

She'd found the recipe in an old, leather-bound book at the antique store, its pages yellowed and brittle. The title read: *"The Yuletide Treat: A Recipe for Festive Delight."* Mom said it was perfect—unique, traditional, and sure to impress the judges.

Something about the book unsettled me. The illustrations were odd, almost alive, and the directions were strangely specific, with phrases like "knead with intention" and "whisper your wishes to the batter." But Mom laughed off my concerns.

"It's just an old recipe," she said, sprinkling sugar into the mixing bowl. "What's the harm?"

The cake was massive, its layers towering over the kitchen counter. The frosting was deep crimson, like fresh berries, and the decorations were eerily lifelike—miniature candy people with intricate features and expressions. When Mom finished, she stepped back, her face glowing with pride.

"It's beautiful," she said. "Isn't it?"

I nodded, but I couldn't shake the feeling that the cake was... watching me.

That night, I woke to the sound of faint, rhythmic tapping. At first, I thought it was just the wind, but as I listened, the sound grew louder, more deliberate. It was coming from the kitchen.

I crept downstairs, my heart pounding. The house was dark, but the faint glow of the Christmas tree lights cast eerie shadows on the walls.

The cake was still there, sitting on the counter. But something was wrong.

The candy people had moved.

They were no longer standing in neat, decorative rows. Some had toppled over, while others had turned their tiny faces toward me. Their sugary eyes glinted in the dim light, and their expressions seemed to shift—smiling one moment, scowling the next.

A sharp crack broke the silence. One of the candy figures fell, shattering against the counter. But instead of crumbs and sugar, a thick, dark liquid oozed from the broken pieces.

It wasn't frosting. It was blood.

I stumbled back, my breath catching in my throat. The cake seemed to tremble, its layers quivering as if alive. The frosting rippled, and the candy people twitched, their limbs jerking in unnatural movements.

And then, the cake *opened*.

The top layer split like a mouth, revealing rows of jagged, sugar-coated teeth. A low, guttural growl echoed through the kitchen as the cake began to move, dragging itself across the counter with frosting-covered tendrils.

I screamed, running back upstairs to wake my mom. But when I reached her room, she was gone. The bed was empty, the sheets rumpled. A faint trail of frosting led out the door.

"Mom!" I yelled, my voice cracking.

The growling grew louder, followed by a sickening crunch. I turned toward the stairs just in time to see the cake dragging something up from the floor. A hand—my mom's hand—emerged from the frosting, clutching at the air before being pulled back inside.

I froze, too terrified to move as the cake turned toward me. Its candy people crawled across its surface, their tiny faces twisted in malevolent glee.

"Join us," the cake rumbled, its voice thick and wet. "The feast must grow."

I bolted out the door, into the freezing night. Behind me, the house filled with the sound of breaking glass and splintering wood as the cake pursued me, its frosting tendrils scraping against the walls.

I ran until my legs gave out, collapsing in the snow outside the town square. When I looked back, the cake was gone. The house stood silent and dark, as if nothing had happened.

But the next morning, the town awoke to horror.

The Christmas Cake contest tent was empty, the tables overturned, and the other contestants missing. In the center of the square stood a massive, grotesque cake. Its layers dripped with crimson frosting, and its decorations were no longer candy people.

They were faces. Human faces, frozen in expressions of terror.

No one entered the square that day. By nightfall, the cake was gone, leaving only a faint trail of frosting and blood.

This year, the contest was canceled. But sometimes, late at night, I hear it—the faint sound of tapping, followed by a low, hungry growl.

And I know the Christmas Cake is still out there, waiting for its next feast.

22. The Christmas Cake

It started as a holiday baking tradition in our small town of Everpine. Every year, the town held a Christmas Cake contest, where families and bakeries would compete to make the most extravagant and delicious cake. This year, my mom was determined to win.

She'd found the recipe in an old, leather-bound book at the antique store, its pages yellowed and brittle. The title read: *"The Yuletide Treat: A Recipe for Festive Delight."* Mom said it was perfect—unique, traditional, and sure to impress the judges.

Something about the book unsettled me. The illustrations were odd, almost alive, and the directions were strangely specific, with phrases like "knead with intention" and "whisper your wishes to the batter." But Mom laughed off my concerns.

"It's just an old recipe," she said, sprinkling sugar into the mixing bowl. "What's the harm?"

The cake was massive, its layers towering over the kitchen counter. The frosting was deep crimson, like fresh berries, and the decorations were eerily lifelike—miniature candy people with intricate features and expressions. When Mom finished, she stepped back, her face glowing with pride.

"It's beautiful," she said. "Isn't it?"

I nodded, but I couldn't shake the feeling that the cake was... watching me.

That night, I woke to the sound of faint, rhythmic tapping. At first, I thought it was just the wind, but as I listened, the sound grew louder, more deliberate. It was coming from the kitchen.

I crept downstairs, my heart pounding. The house was dark, but the faint glow of the Christmas tree lights cast eerie shadows on the walls.

The cake was still there, sitting on the counter. But something was wrong.

The candy people had moved.

They were no longer standing in neat, decorative rows. Some had toppled over, while others had turned their tiny faces toward me. Their sugary eyes glinted in the dim light, and their expressions seemed to shift—smiling one moment, scowling the next.

A sharp crack broke the silence. One of the candy figures fell, shattering against the counter. But instead of crumbs and sugar, a thick, dark liquid oozed from the broken pieces.

It wasn't frosting. It was blood.

I stumbled back, my breath catching in my throat. The cake seemed to tremble, its layers quivering as if alive. The frosting rippled, and the candy people twitched, their limbs jerking in unnatural movements.

And then, the cake *opened*.

The top layer split like a mouth, revealing rows of jagged, sugar-coated teeth. A low, guttural growl echoed through the kitchen as the cake began to move, dragging itself across the counter with frosting-covered tendrils.

I screamed, running back upstairs to wake my mom. But when I reached her room, she was gone. The bed was empty, the sheets rumpled. A faint trail of frosting led out the door.

"Mom!" I yelled, my voice cracking.

The growling grew louder, followed by a sickening crunch. I turned toward the stairs just in time to see the cake dragging something up from the floor. A hand—my mom's hand—emerged from the frosting, clutching at the air before being pulled back inside.

I froze, too terrified to move as the cake turned toward me. Its candy people crawled across its surface, their tiny faces twisted in malevolent glee.

"Join us," the cake rumbled, its voice thick and wet. "The feast must grow."

I bolted out the door, into the freezing night. Behind me, the house filled with the sound of breaking glass and splintering wood as the cake pursued me, its frosting tendrils scraping against the walls.

I ran until my legs gave out, collapsing in the snow outside the town square. When I looked back, the cake was gone. The house stood silent and dark, as if nothing had happened.

But the next morning, the town awoke to horror.

The Christmas Cake contest tent was empty, the tables overturned, and the other contestants missing. In the center of the square stood a massive, grotesque cake. Its layers dripped with crimson frosting, and its decorations were no longer candy people.

They were faces. Human faces, frozen in expressions of terror.

No one entered the square that day. By nightfall, the cake was gone, leaving only a faint trail of frosting and blood.

This year, the contest was canceled. But sometimes, late at night, I hear it—the faint sound of tapping, followed by a low, hungry growl.

And I know the Christmas Cake is still out there, waiting for its next feast.

23.The Frostling

Every year, my small town of Wintershade held a Christmas Eve festival, complete with carolers, a tree-lighting ceremony, and hot cocoa stands. But there was one rule everyone followed without question:

Never build a snowman after midnight.

It was a silly tradition, or so I thought. When I asked my mom about it, she avoided the question, her expression darkening. The only explanation I ever got came from Old Man Griggs, the town recluse.

"They come alive after midnight," he said one day, leaning heavily on his cane. His voice was low, his tone grave. "If you're lucky, they'll just watch you. If you're not…"

He didn't finish, but the scar across his face said enough.

Of course, my friends and I didn't believe him. We were teenagers, and rules were meant to be broken. That's why, last Christmas Eve, we decided to test the legend.

The festival ended around 11 PM, and by the time we gathered on the edge of the park, the town was quiet. The snow was untouched, glittering under the pale moonlight. Armed with scarves, hats, and an arsenal of mischief, we got to work.

Our snowman was enormous. We rolled massive snowballs for the base, middle, and head, stacking them precariously. We gave him stick arms, coal eyes, and a crooked carrot nose. It was almost 12:30 AM by the time we finished.

"He's perfect," Jake said, stepping back to admire our work. "The Frostling."

"Terrifying," I joked, snapping a picture with my phone. The snowman looked harmless—almost goofy with its lopsided grin.

But then the air changed.

The wind died suddenly, leaving an eerie stillness in its wake. The temperature plummeted, and the hairs on the back of my neck stood up.

"Guys," Lily whispered. "Do you hear that?"

At first, I thought it was just the crunch of snow under our boots. But then I realized the sound was coming from the snowman.

A soft, rhythmic creaking, like ice shifting on a frozen lake.

"Very funny," I said, rolling my eyes at Jake. "Who rigged it?"

But Jake looked just as confused—and scared—as I felt.

The snowman's head tilted. Slowly. The coal eyes seemed to sink deeper into its face, and the crooked grin widened unnaturally, splitting the snow like a jagged crack.

"What the hell?" Lily gasped, stumbling back.

Before any of us could move, the snowman's arms shot out. The sticks splintered and elongated, turning into claw-like icicles. It lurched forward, its massive body moving with a horrifying fluidity, like the snow itself was alive.

Jake screamed as one of its clawed hands wrapped around his leg, dragging him down. He thrashed, kicking at the snow, but his foot sank deeper into the freezing grip.

"Help me!" he cried, his voice choking on terror.

We grabbed his arms, pulling with everything we had. But the snow-man was too strong. It let out a low, guttural sound—a laugh that didn't belong in this world. Jake's screams cut off as the snow engulfed him, swallowing him whole. In seconds, he was gone.

The Frostling turned toward us, its grin now wide enough to split its head in two. The coal eyes glowed faintly, and it took another step for-ward.

"Run!" I shouted, grabbing Lily's arm.

We sprinted through the park, the sound of creaking snow and cracking ice following close behind. I didn't dare look back, but I could feel it—feel its eyes boring into me.

We made it to Lily's house and slammed the door behind us, locking it tight. For hours, we sat huddled in the dark, listening to the faint crunch of snow outside the window. When dawn finally came, the sound stopped.

Jake was never found. The town called it a tragic accident, blaming thin ice on the frozen lake. But Lily and I knew the truth.

This year, the festival feels different. The townsfolk are quieter, more cautious. And every night since the first snowfall, I've felt it watching me.

The Frostling isn't just a story. It's real. And it's waiting for someone foolish enough to build another snowman after midnight.

Don't make the same mistake we did.

<u>Message from the Author:</u>

I hope you enjoyed this book, I love astrology and knew there was not a book such as this out on the shelf. I love metaphysical items as well. Please check out my other books:

-Life of Government Benefits

-My life of Hell

-My life with Hydrocephalus

-Red Sky

-World Domination:Woman's rule

-World Domination:Woman's Rule 2: The War

-Life and Banishment of Apophis: book 1

-The Kidney Friendly Diet

-The Ultimate Hemp Cookbook

-Creating a Dispensary(legally)

-Cleanliness throughout life: the importance of showering from childhood to adulthood.

-Strong Roots: The Risks of Overcoddling children

-Hemp Horoscopes: Cosmic Insights and Earthly Healing

- Celestial Hemp Navigating the Zodiac: Through the Green Cosmos

-Astrological Hemp: Aligning The Stars with Earth's Ancient Herb

-The Astrological Guide to Hemp: Stars, Signs, and Sacred Leaves

-Green Growth: Innovative Marketing Strategies for your Hemp Products and Dispensary

-Cosmic Cannabis

-Astrological Munchies

-Henry The Hemp

-Zodiacal Roots: The Astrological Soul Of Hemp

- **Green Constellations: Intersection of Hemp and Zodiac**

-Hemp in The Houses: An astrological Adventure Through The Cannabis Galaxy

-Galactic Ganja Guide

Heavenly Hemp
Zodiac Leaves
Doctor Who Astrology
Cannastrology
Stellar Satvias and Cosmic Indicas
<u>Celestial Cannabis: A Zodiac Journey</u>
AstroHerbology: The Sky and The Soil: Volume 1
AstroHerbology:Celestial Cannabis:Volume 2
Cosmic Cannabis Cultivation
The Starry Guide to Herbal Harmony: Volume 1
The Starry Guide to Herbal Harmony: Cannabis Universe: Volume
2
Yugioh Astrology: Astrological Guide to Deck, Duels and more
Nightmare Mansion: Echoes of The Abyss
Nightmare Mansion 2: Legacy of Shadows
Nightmare Mansion 3: Shadows of the Forgotten
Nightmare Mansion 4: Echoes of the Damned
The Life and Banishment of Apophis: Book 2
Nightmare Mansion: Halls of Despair
<u>Healing with Herb: Cannabis and Hydrocephalus</u>
<u>Planetary Pot: Aligning with Astrological Herbs: Volume 1</u>
Fast Track to Freedom: 30 Days to Financial Independence Using AI, Assets, and Agile Hustles
<u>Cosmic Hemp Pathways</u>
How to Become Financially Free in 30 Days: 10,000 Paths to Prosperity
Zodiacal Herbage: Astrological Insights: Volume 1
Nightmare Mansion: Whispers in the Walls
The Daleks Invade Atlantis
Henry the hemp and Hydrocephalus

10X The Kidney Friendly Diet
Cannabis Universe: Adult coloring book

Hemp Astrology: The Healing Power of the Stars

Zodiacal Herbage: Astrological Insights: Cannabis Universe: Volume 2

<u>Planetary Pot: Aligning with Astrological Herbs: Cannabis Universes: Volume 2</u>

Doctor Who Meets the Replicators and SG-1: The Ultimate Battle for Survival

Nightmare Mansion: Curse of the Blood Moon

<u>The Celestial Stoner: A Guide to the Zodiac</u>

Cosmic Pleasures: Sex Toy Astrology for Every Sign

Hydrocephalus Astrology: Navigating the Stars and Healing Waters

Lapis and the Mischievous Chocolate Bar

Celestial Positions: Sexual Astrology for Every Sign

Apophis's Shadow Work Journal: : A Journey of Self-Discovery and Healing

Kinky Cosmos: Sexual Kink Astrology for Every Sign

Digital Cosmos: The Astrological Digimon Compendium

Stellar Seeds: The Cosmic Guide to Growing with Astrology

Apophis's Daily Gratitude Journal

Cat Astrology: Feline Mysteries of the Cosmos

The Cosmic Kama Sutra: An Astrological Guide to Sexual Positions

Unleash Your Potential: A Guided Journal Powered by AI Insights

Whispers of the Enchanted Grove

Cosmic Pleasures: An Astrological Guide to Sexual Kinks

369, 12 Manifestation Journal

Whisper of the nocturne journal(blank journal for writing or drawing)

The Boogey Book

Locked In Reflection: A Chastity Journey Through Locktober

Generating Wealth Quickly:

How to Generate $100,000 in 24 Hours

Star Magic: Harness the Power of the Universe

The Flatulence Chronicles: A Fart Journal for Self-Discovery

The Doctor and The Death Moth

Seize the Day: A Personal Seizure Tracking Journal

The Ultimate Boogeyman Safari: A Journey into the Boogie World and Beyond

Whispers of Samhain: 1,000 Spells of Love, Luck, and Lunar Magic: Samhain Spell Book

Apophis's guides:

Witch's Spellbook Crafting Guide for Halloween

<u>Frost & Flame: The Enchanted Yule Grimoire of 1000 Winter Spells</u>

<u>The Ultimate Boogey Goo Guide & Spooky Activities for Halloween Fun</u>

Harmony of the Scales: A Libra's Spellcraft for Balance and Beauty

The Enchanted Advent: 36 Days of Christmas Wonders

Nightmare Mansion: The Labyrinth of Screams

Harvest of Enchantment: 1,000 Spells of Gratitude, Love, and Fortune for Thanksgiving

The Boogey Chronicles: A Journal of Nightly Encounters and Shadowy Secrets

The 12 Days of Financial Freedom: A Step-by-Step Christmas Countdown to Transform Your Finances

Sigil of the Eternal Spiral Blank Journal

A Christmas Feast: Timeless Recipes for Every Meal

Holiday Stress-Free Solutions: A Survival Guide to Thriving During the Festive Season

Yu-Gi-Oh! Holiday Gifting Mastery: The Ultimate Guide for Fans and Newcomers Alike

Holiday Harmony: A Hydrocephalus Survival Guide for the Festive Season

Celestial Craft: The Witch's Almanac for 2025 – A Cosmic Guide to Manifestations, Moons, and Mystical Events

Doctor Who: The Toymaker's Winter Wonderland

Tulsa King Unveiled: A Thrilling Guide to Stallone's Mafia Masterpiece

Pendulum Craft: A Complete Guide to Crafting and Using Personalized Divination Tools

Nightmare Mansion: Santa's Eternal Eve

Starlight Noel: A Cosmic Journey through Christmas Mysteries

The Dark Architect: Unlocking the Blueprint of Existence

Surviving the Embrace: The Ultimate Guide to Encounters with The Hugging Molly

The Enchanted Codex: Secrets of the Craft for Witches, Wiccans, and Pagans

Harvest of Gratitude: A Complete Thanksgiving Guide

Yuletide Essentials: A Complete Guide to an Authentic and Magical Christmas

Celestial Smokes: A Cosmic Guide to Cigars and Astrology

Living in Balance: A Comprehensive Survival Guide to Thriving with Diabetes Insipidus

Cosmic Symbiosis: The Venom Zodiac Chronicles

The Cursed Paw of Ambition

Cosmic Symbiosis: The Astrological Venom Journal

Celestial Wonders Unfold: A Stargazer's Guide to the Cosmos (2024-2029)

The Ultimate Black Friday Prepper's Guide: Mastering Shopping Strategies and Savings

Cosmic Sales: The Astrological Guide to Black Friday Shopping

Legends of the Corn Mother and Other Harvest Myths

Whispers of the Harvest: The Corn Mother's Journal

The Evergreen Spellbook

The Doctor Meets the Boogeyman

The White Witch of Rose Hall's SpellBook

The Gingerbread Golem's Shadow: A Study in Sweet Darkness

The Gingerbread Golem Codex: An Academic Exploration of Sweet Myths

The Gingerbread Golem Grimoire: Sweet Magicks and Spells for the Festive Witch

The Curse of the Gingerbread Golem

10-minute Christmas Crafts for kids

<u>Christmas Crisis Solutions: The Ultimate Last-Minute Survival Guide</u>

Gingerbread Golem Recipes: Holiday Treats with a Magical Twist

The Infinite Key: Unlocking Mystical Secrets of the Ages

Enchanted Yule: A Wiccan and Pagan Guide to a Magical and Memorable Season

Dinosaurs of Power: Unlocking Ancient Magick

Astro-Dinos: The Cosmic Guide to Prehistoric Wisdom

Gallifrey's Yule Logs: A Festive Doctor Who Cookbook

The Dino Grimoire: Secrets of Prehistoric Magick

The Gift They Never Knew They Needed

The Gingerbread Golem's Culinary Alchemy: Enchanting Recipes for a Sweetly Dark Feast

A Time Lord Christmas: Holiday Adventures with the Doctor

Krampusproofing Your Home: Defensive Strategies for Yule

If you want solar for your home go here: https://www.harborso-lar.live/apophisenterprises/

Get Some Tarot cards: https://www.makeplayingcards.com/sell/apophis-occult-shop

<u>Get some shirts: https://www.bonfire.com/store/apophis-shirt-emporium/</u>

<u>**Instagrams:**</u>
@apophis_enterprises,
@apophisbookemporium,
@apophisscardshop
Twitter: @apophisenterpr1
Tiktok:@apophisenterprise
Youtube: @sg1fan23477, @FiresideRetreatKingdom
Hive: @sg1fan23477
CheeLee: @SG1fan23477

Podcast: Apophis Chat Zone: https://open.spotify.com/show/5zXbrCLEV2xzCp8ybrfHsk?si=fb4d4fdbdce44dec

Newsletter: https://apophiss-newsletter-27c897.beehiiv.com/